GO AWAY,
UNICORN!

For my sisters Leigh-Anne and Lindsay

First published in Canada by McKellar & Martin Publishing Group, Ltd.,
at 1114 Dublin Street, New Westminster, BC V3M 2Y9.

Text and illustrations copyright © 2010 by Emily Mullock

The publisher does not have any control over and does not assume any
responsibility for author or third-party websites or their content.

This book is a work of fiction. Names, characters, places, and incidents are either the product
of the author's imagination or are used fictitiously, and any resemblance to actual persons,
living or dead, business establishments, events, or locales is entirely coincidental.

ISBN 978-1-338-57571-2

10 9 8 7 6 5 4 3 2 1   19 20 21 22 23

Printed in Malaysia 108
This edition first printing, September 2019

GO AWAY, UNICORN!

Text & illustrations by
EMILY MULLOCK

SCHOLASTIC INC.

Alice met the unicorn at her tenth birthday party in the park.

He had not been invited.

The unicorn had come because he'd smelled cake (his *most* favorite food).

He stayed because he'd seen Alice.

Now, you have to be pretty dumb to think that Alice was a unicorn just because of her shiny, gold party hat.

But unicorns can be pretty dumb.

Her friend Patty said, "You got
a unicorn for your birthday??!!
All I got was a boring goldfish."

Alice shrugged. She had no use for a unicorn.

Even so, the unicorn played party games,
he gave rides on his back, and he let
everyone pet his luxurious, sparkly mane.

But when the party was over, and everyone
had gone home, the unicorn was still there.

Alice said,

"GO AWAY, UNICORN."

But unicorns aren't very good listeners.

Alice was not pleased that the unicorn had followed her home. "This is silly," she said, and took off her party hat. "See? I'm not some weird horse. I can't be your friend."

Alice frowned. She said,

"GO AWAY, UNICORN."

But unicorns know a friend
when they see one.
So, the unicorn moved in.

He made a nest for himself in her bedroom.
He used pages from Alice's favorite books
and some old, shiny wrapping paper.
He was very comfortable.

He ate her cereal – but only the tiny,
pink marshmallows, which were, of course,
the best part.

He used all of her shampoo
to wash his mane . . .

. . . Alice said,

"GO AWAY, UNICORN."

But unicorns are easily distracted.
The unicorn hogged the remote.
He tracked glitter through the house.
He snored all night.
And he followed Alice to school.

. . . Alice said,

"GO AWAY, UNICORN."

But unicorns can be very sneaky.

Alice's teacher asked,
"Where is your homework?"
"My unicorn ate it," Alice replied.

That unicorn just would not go.

Alice tried to tell him he was a mythical creature. "That means you don't exist," she explained.

But that just made the unicorn feel more special.

She tried to lose him in the park, but he just thought it was a game.

She tried to ship him to the zoo, but the zookeeper said, "I'm sorry. Unicorns don't exist."

"I know that!" Alice cried, and buried her head in her hands.

The unicorn could tell something was wrong.

It's a good thing unicorns know just how to cheer up a friend.

The unicorn turned Alice's hair bright pink. Pink was his *most* favorite color.

Pink made Alice want to throw up.

Alice had had enough.

She stared at her hair.
She stared at the unicorn.

She said the meanest thing
she could think of:

"You are *so* not my friend.
I would rather have a goldfish than you!"

Even unicorns know when
they're being insulted.
So the unicorn left.
And he did not come back.

It was very quiet with no snoring.

And it was very dull with no glitter.

And it was very plain in Alice's house with no pink.

But most of all, it was very lonely with no best friend.

Alice might not have known a lot about being best friends, but she was pretty sure that the unicorn was doing a lot better job of it than she was.

Alice whispered,

"COME BACK, UNICORN."

Unicorns have very good hearing.

Alice hugged her unicorn. She said, "Sometimes even best friends fight."

Unicorns know an apology when they hear one.